A Kitten in My Closet

RM Morrissey

First Published 2022 by RM Morrissey

ISBN: 9798403969116

Copyright © RM Morrissey, 2022

A CIP catalogue record for this book is available from the British Library.

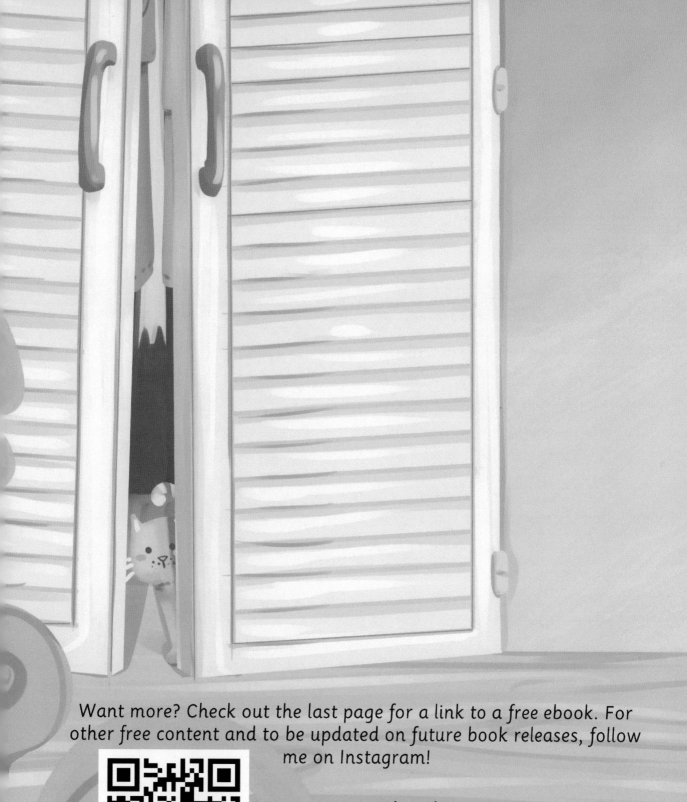

Want more? Check out the last page for a link to a free ebook. For other free content and to be updated on future book releases, follow me on Instagram!

@rmorrisseybooks

My cat, her name is Mittens.
She hides in my closet, you see.
For my friends, they all like dogs,
and they're as proud as can be.

I'm nervous to tell them,
for they are my friends,
that sure, dogs are wonderful,
but Mittens is mine to the end.

It all started weeks ago. It made me upset. It made me doubt. My friends, they all got puppies, and I started to feel left out.

I asked my mum, "Please,
oh pretty please, with a cherry on top?"
I hugged and kissed and begged,
and everything - I just wouldn't stop!

But the dog that I asked for -
ended up being a kitten instead.
It's like she didn't listen
to a single word that I said.

This cat wasn't what I begged for,
but I named her Mittens anyway.
I was annoyed that she wasn't a puppy
but was a little ginger cat to stay.

Meow

I gave it a chance though.
It was something to do.
And besides, it's not often
that you get something new.

I quickly learnt that cats
could be fun in their own little way.
They were different of course,
but that doesn't matter, I say.

We played, and we played
all through the weekend.
Mittens was mine,
my little ginger kitten.

But my friends, they loved dogs.
"They're way better than cats!"
My stomach, it did backflips each
time they said that.

So, Mittens had to hide
whenever they were around.
This went on for a while,
and she was never found.

Mittens was my little secret
to keep and hold dear.
I didn't think that this secret
would cause me such fear.

One day, after school,
everything changed.
My secret got out,
let me explain ...

We stopped at Abdul's house
to visit his puppy named Zoom.
And oh boy! What a mess!
What a sight! What a room!

They ran and they jumped
over couches and chairs,
knocking over lamps,
destruction everywhere.

Then we went to Kacey's house,
and wow! It was loud!
His puppy named Screech
could sure draw a crowd.

He sang and he sang
at the top of his puppy-dog lungs.
But after a while, it sounded
like the banging of drums.

With our heads filled with ringing,
we went on our way
to Lawrence's house
for a nap and to stay

with his puppy named Floofy
who just loved to cuddle.
Yes, Floofy is my favourite.
She doesn't cause any trouble!

When we got to my house,
I had my friends wait by the stairs.
I had to hide Mittens or
else they'd be aware

that I had a cat,
something they didn't like.
Yes, they are my friends,
but this is something that might

make them think that I'm different,
or that I might not be cool.
To be different is scary
with your friends here from school.

WILL THEY HATE ME?

WHAT SHOULD I DO?

WHAT WILL THEY SAY?

What might they say?
What might they share?
Mittens is my secret.
Could I possibly dare

to show her to them?
Would they understand?
Or will I end up alone
with Mittens as my only friend?

We chilled in my room

like we usually did,

and everything was great,

because Mittens was hid

in the closet where

they couldn't find ...

but to hide a secret in a closet?

Was I out of my mind?

I'm such a fool

to think that she'd hide there all day,

that she'd keep quiet and out of the way.

No, she's a kitten, and she wanted to play!

She jumped out at Kacey,
right into his arms.
My face, it went white.
It was filled with alarm.

It was like time stood still.
Everything went grey ...
"Oh no!" I was thinking,
"What will they say?"

Kacey cuddled Mittens,

squished her ears and her nose.

He tickled her belly,

and he tickled her toes.

"Oh, a kitten! So cute!

A little ginger cat!

I wanted one, but Dad's allergic,

or something like that.

So, now I've got Screech

who rattles my ears.

I love that dog dearly,

but he brings me to tears!"

Lawrence scooched over
and gave Mittens a cuddle.
She really liked him and
moved in close for a snuggle.

"You've got a kitten.
Oh, you're so lucky!

I wanted one too,
but I was allowed only one pet.
So, it was Floofy
I chose and yet,

maybe if I'm good,
right down to the bone ...
Maybe I'll be allowed
a little ginger cat of my own!"

They looked at me puzzled.
They thought for a sec ...
I was shaking in my boots
and sweat dripped down my neck.

"Why didn't you tell us
that you had a kitten?
Why did you keep her
in the closet all hidden?"

"I - uh - well, you said
that you didn't like cats.
And that made me worried.
I was worried that ...
Well, I don't actually know.
I guess - I guess it was silly."

"We don't like cats?
What made you think that?"

"Well, I guess that's something
That we did say,
but that's only because Abdul
got bit on the way

to the park when he was coming
to meet us, you see.
Yes, it's just that mean cat.
Abdul, you agree?"

"Abdul! You're quiet.
Come, see the kitten.
Give her a cuddle,
and I'm sure you'll be smitten."

"Don't worry, she's not like
that mean cat from the street.
Here, why don't you give
Mittens a treat?"

It took Abdul some days
before he changed his view.
He was still scared of cats,
this much was true.

And who could blame him,
he was bitten so hard
by a stray cat on the streets
which has left his hand scarred.

Abdul didn't hate cats,
though he was afraid.
It was a secret he kept,
a secret that made

him change how he acted,

what he said and he did.

A secret like mine,

from our friends that we hid.

We held our secrets close.
We kept them inside.
Where no one could find them
even if they tried.

Mine made me worried
that I'd lose my friends.
And Abdul's ... well,
he didn't intend

to make me feel worried,
scared like I did,
to keep Mittens inside
a closet all hid.

He was trying to be cool,
calm and collected,
but really, deep inside,
he was affected

more than we knew,
over something so small.
Something we knew nothing of,
nothing at all.

Sometimes a secret
can be big or be small.
Sometimes it can really
be nothing at all.

But it's in our friends
that we put our trust,
It's with our friends that we should
feel comfortable enough

to share and be understood.
Though at times it might be scary,
we have to be strong,
because a closet is not where a kitten belongs.

ACKNOWLEDGMENTS

Thank you to all of the children who have given me excellent feedback on the many, many many versions of this book. It has been a wonderful experience working with you, listening to your likes and dislikes.

Children truly make excellent editors!

If you enjoyed reading the book, consider following me on Instagram for links to free content and to be updated on future book releases.

@rmorrisseybooks

Want More?

Download a FREE ebook
written by RM Morrissey

FREE ebook!

https://linktr.ee/rmorrisseybooks

Printed in Great Britain
by Amazon